The Garden

Magnus Florin

translated by Harry Watson

Vagabond Voices
Glasgow

Translation copyright © Vagabond Voices Publishing Ltd.
May 2014

© Magnus Florin 2014

First published in May 2014 by
Vagabond Voices Publishing Ltd.,
Glasgow,
Scotland.

ISBN 978-1-908251-26-8

The author's right to be identified as author of this book under the Copyright, Designs and Patents Act 1988 has been asserted.

Printed and bound in Poland

Cover design by Mark Mechan

Typeset by Park Productions

For further information on Vagabond Voices, see the website, www.vagabondvoices.co.uk

The Garden

This happened. A meeting on the first day, the first hour. Petrus Arctædius, from Nordmaling, and Carl Linnæus, from Småland. The first handshake was followed by animated conversation about stones, plants and animals. Observations were exchanged and what the one did not know, the other did not hesitate to tell him. They were like two siblings. Arctædius the big brother, Linnæus two years younger.

They drank sloe wine, ate cream and made up their own songs. "Two friends were sitting. In artless repooooose …" Arctædius was a good singer. Alongside him, Linnæus was emboldened to join in the tune. From time to time they dropped off from drunkenness and exhaustion. Woke up and carried on singing.

They imagined everything in the world divided into two halves. The hard things in one half and the soft things in another. The fixed and the moveable. The annual and the perennial. What had no tail and what had a tail. That which was fast and that which was slow. The two-legged and the four-legged. The hairy and the hairless.

They imagined each of these halves divided in

turn into two new halves. And so on into further divisions, with no end in sight.

This delighted and astonished them.

Growing friendship between the hesitant, serious Arctædius and Linnæus, small and lively. The tall, gaunt Arctædius and the hasty, fidgety Linnæus. The restless Linnæus and the watchful Arctædius, inclined towards procrastination yet first to reach the target due to the thoroughness of his preparations. The enterprising Linnæus and the patient Arctædius.

An odd couple. Their dialects differed. Yet each one a mirror image of the other. They competed and their rivalry was a game. But one day there was an intimation of discord. "It was I who …" "You …?" "Yes indeed." "You're joking, it was I who …"

They decided to divide up the field of study. It was a separation agreed on by both of them. Arctædius took the amphibians, the reptiles, the frogs and toads and the fish. Linnæus took the birds and the insects, the mammals and the stones. Along with the plants. But Arctædius got the *Umbelliferæ* family as he had a new method planned for them.

Linnæus did not like the cold, slippery fish.

Linnæus brown-eyed. His friend's eyes light blue.

They promised each other that if one of them died, the other would regard it as a sacred duty to transmit to the world the observations which the deceased had left behind him.

It is muddy autumn. It is not warm, it is not cold. The gardener feels the soil between his thumb and middle finger. He smells it, tastes it. It is the salt sea. It is the black clay of the Uppsala plain. He strolls, as he is in the habit of doing, round the squares of the plant beds. He rakes dry leaves from the paths. He puts the rake in the tool shed and falls asleep inside, waiting. He is woken by a cloudburst. It is Thursday morning and time for the cheese and butter delivery from Hallkved.

The gardener exchanges a few words with the coachman and the servant, who are soaked by the driving rain. They laugh together. They yawn. They stand silent, looking out over the plain, the clay, and over towards the cornfields.

They think about porridge, gruel, bread. They stand silent, still. It is a long drawn-out moment.

But a change comes and the two of them show signs of departing, take their places in the cart and drive on towards Lövsta.

The gardener stands with the butter and cheese in his arms and looks after them. Then he walks in the direction of the subterranean larder.

The friends Linnæus and Arctædius studied the *Umbelliferæ* together.

They are: the umbelliferous plants. Chervil. Wild chervil. Shepherd's needle. Hemlock. Upright hedge parsley. Slender hare's-ear. Carrot. Hogweed. Water fennel. Lesser water parsnip. Cumin. Pennywort.

Arctædius had a slender hare's-ear in front of him:
"Bluish-green, slender, branching from its base.

Leaves like narrow lancets, without indentations. Umbels with few flowers, the upper one composite, with three involucres. The others simple from the axil, with involucres longer than the umbel. The fruit round, with small spines and narrow ridges."

Linnæus is out in the wind on the Uppsala plain, waiting for the carriage from the coaching establishment at Böksta. Linnæus is in his chamber, dressing.

Linnæus cannot help being Linnæus.

Obviously Linnæus buttons up the twenty-five buttonholes in his waistcoat with his own fingers. He fastens the buttons with the thumbs, index fingers and middle fingers of both hands, and is careful not to fasten them unevenly. He can begin from the top or the bottom – in this he allows himself a bit of variety – but never in the middle. Beginning in the middle is only advisable with shirts, which never have more than seventeen buttons, but even with them he finds it more convenient to begin from the bottom or the top. In fact, he usually sets about it from the top, for the simple reason that it is difficult to see the lower buttonholes and buttons in the mirror.

Now he is fastening the twenty-eight buttons in the long green camlet coat and taking care not to fasten them unevenly.

Now he tosses up the twenty-five and the twenty-eight buttons high above his head and he will not get them back.

Now, if you must be Linnæus.

Linnæus is out in the wind on the Uppsala plain, waiting to set off, with his large bag in his hand.

He lifts the bag high in the air: take this bag! But nobody takes the bag out of his hands and he remains standing. The wind blows and he feels it blowing.

But now he tosses up the twenty-eight youths, the twenty-eight disciples, into the wind on the Uppsala plain, and they are scattered.

Arctædius set out his best idea for his friend: the genera must somehow be arranged into maniples and their orders would then emerge of their own accord.

"This is all chaos at present."

But the art of creating order also involves the ability to set limits to the ordering.

"The distinction between fixed species and random difference must be maintained."

Linnæus is at home in this world. He searches, all by himself, for an important passage in a work in progress simply to give himself a pretext for perusing all his papers. He directs shrieks of dissatisfaction at his writing materials. He walks up and down in irritation. He drums on the desk with his fingers. He flings himself on the bed, snorting.

These are all regular affectations. Actually he is content. Often he needs only to linger a little by the glass panes of the cabinets and to gaze at the vessels behind them to feel at peace.

But today that is not enough. There is a stirring of unease in his body.

He goes into the instrument room and over to the window that looks out onto the garden. It is his garden, which he has laid out. Beside the window, close by the frame, he has placed a map of the garden. "Plan" would perhaps be a more accurate word. He sees, and rejoices over, the congruity between the garden in the picture and the real garden.

The gardener is moving about outside, this way and that, to and fro. It seems arbitrary. Occasionally he falls over, but gets up again immediately. He struggles forward, as if into a headwind. He walks with a firm stride, then suddenly staggers and falls headlong, or chooses a new direction and walks on.

Linnæus pulls a face behind the windowpane, waves, and tries to attract the gardener's attention with a "Hallooo!" He wants the gardener to stop, perhaps take a break, pull off his shoes and see to his toes and the soles of his feet, as he usually does. But the gardener carries on.

Linnæus thinks: his continual, everlasting motion!

Now there is a ceremony or display, like in a salon. First figure: *le pantalon*. Then *l'été*. Third figure: *la poule*. After that *la pastourelle*. Finally the fifth figure: *le final*.

Linnæus finds this admirable. A round of applause would be in order. But the gardener dances on into something else. Linnæus remains standing at the window and watches a strange ballet, quite absurd.

The windowpane is dirty. It has been cleaned recently, but the dirt has not been removed and in the process of rinsing it has dried out in the pattern of a wave. It has an unexpectedly artistic appearance. Linnæus gazes at it. When he looks out again, the gardener is gone.

Arctædius began by putting his name in order. His brothers and sisters said Petter, although his baptismal name was Petrus. He preferred Peter himself. He simplified his family name to Artedius. Then to Artedi. So, Peter Artedi.

Then he proudly counted the fish he had dissected and described, "Mackerel, pike-perch, bream. Perch, asp, flounder. Flying fish, grayling, ide. Four-horned sculpin, bleak, shorthorn sculpin.

Linnæus to his friend: "The subjects of your favourite discipline are not all to be found in the River Fyris. They are spread over the whole world. You won't be staying."

"I'll be staying," said Artedi.

Linnæus applied for a post in the Uppsala garden. He knew that he possessed the best qualifications and counted on getting the post. But he didn't. Rudbeck took on someone else and Linnæus, upset, went to him for an explanation.

"Yes. You would be the best person to keep the waters of the Svartbäck flowing. Yes. I see that you are angry. You would be the best. But this is not what you should be doing. You should stay away from Uppsala garden. It is not for you. You should not occupy yourself with unskilled labour."

Linnæus:

"There is no longer any creation; life continues as it was given. There are no more species today than there were before. So if life continues thus in every generation, it follows that individuals remain unaltered, each one within its own species."

"Take this rake," the gardener says to Linnæus.

Linnæus tries to take it.

"Not like that," says the gardener.

He means: "Take it, take it as an idea, think about it."

But Linnæus cannot think about the rake as an idea. There are so many rakes and so many kinds of rake. Quite definitely one must think of a particular kind of rake: a hay rake, for example, of a particular shape.

The gardener stares hard at Linnæus and says it is a question of this very rake, a rake which must be perceived as a quite definite rake of a quite definite type.

Linnæus says that he is thinking about this rake.

The gardener asks if he is quite sure about that.

Linnæus answers in the affirmative.

The gardener says that Linnæus is to take the rake, yes, really take it in his hand and start raking.

Linnæus does this and rakes away some leaves and some blades of grass from the path. What a lot of leaves and grass there are here, he thinks.

The gardener asks if Linnæus is still thinking about the rake while he is raking. Linnæus says he cannot do that. He has to rake.

Then the gardener says, "There is a difference."

Linnæus asks, "What sort of difference?"

"That," says the gardener, "is the difference."

It's in open countryside. Rainy, and growing steadily colder. Linnæus is sitting at a plain wooden table. Students from Uppsala are standing in a queue, each one with a stone in his hand. They step up, one after the other. First is Höfling:
"Where does this stone come from?"
Linnæus:
"The swampy marsh. Mosses. From there."
Now Hultstedt:
Which place did this stone come from?"
"From there. The wolf moraine."
The students stand in silence, with mild expressions. Orell:
"Where did I get this from?"
Linnæus knows:
"From there. Chalky soil."
Every day he listens to them asking their questions and he can hear from their voices where they come from. Skuttunge. Västerlösa. Levene. Norrby, Lower Norrby.
Now Fougt:
"This one?"
Linnæus knows:
"From there. Sandy soil."
He sees the stones' origins in the landscape. This makes him happy. And his unhappiness, his longing for everything that is not stone and landscape. For his siblings, for his siblings in Småland.
"Here," he says to the students, "here the bedrock emerges into daylight. Feel. *Smell.* Iridescent shale, diorite, porphyry."

In olden days fish used to be divided up according to where they lived: marsh fish, lake fish, river fish, sea fish.

But Artedi laid the foundations for the classification of fish. He divided the flatfish, according to the presence or absence of spines in the dorsal fin, into *Malacopterygii*, those with soft fins, and *Acanthopterygii*, those with spiny fins.

Linnæus, in conversation with Artedi, agreed:

"The advantages of this ought soon to be clear to every ichthyologist."

Rudbeck led Linnæus up the long staircase.

"You will become a teacher, a headmaster, a professor."

Linnæus was ushered into the natural history room with its scrupulously preserved finds.

Rudbeck pointed:

"A flint knife, believed to be a circumcision knife. A stone blackened by nature. The beak of a swordfish. The tooth of a manatee. Ceres carved out of a grain of rice. A Chinese seal of boxwood. A stuffed baby crocodile. A stone in the shape of a bird's head, held by the Lapps to be a divinity. A monstrous *hesperis* with conjoined stalks. A chicken with four feet. A tooth found in a grave in Järlåsa, believed to be an elk's tooth but undoubtedly a giant's tooth from the skull of an authentic giant preserved in Järlåsa church."

Rudbeck on the whole collection:

"Do you see?"

On the way down Rudbeck and Linnæus stood in

the middle of the stone staircase embedded with four hundred fossils.

"Do you see? We expect great things from you."

Stones. The students go on standing. The rain is continuous and cold, but they don't want to leave Linnæus. They want him to show them something, something else.

He says:

"Stones *grow*."

Linnæus is in an excellent humour. He goes down to the garden from his room to talk to the gardener.

"Gardener," says Linnæus, "you have misunderstood everything. You have done things one way and you should have done them another way. You have scratched in the ground the wrong way, you have raked the paths in the wrong direction, you have held the spade the wrong way. But don't let it get you down, don't burst into tears, don't condemn yourself. I will show you how to make everything right again. First I will show you how you did everything wrong, then you will see how it should have been done and how you will do everything correctly from now on."

But the gardener has a musical instrument in his hand. No-one saw where it came from. It wasn't there a moment ago, Linnæus can swear to that, but now it is in the gardener's hand. And suddenly it is in Linnæus's hand.

He turns and twists the instrument. It doesn't look

like much. No-one who was unacquainted with it would be able to comprehend that music could be produced from this piece of wood. Linnæus turns and twists it and thinks it looks attractive.

"Gardener," he says. "I admire your instrument, I am envious of anyone who can play on it. But I can read musical notation, I can understand it."

He tries to give the instrument back to the gardener.

But the gardener is not there, he is somewhere else in the garden now, he has the instrument and Linnæus hears him play. Linnæus tries to drown him out. He shouts to himself, discovers that he is shouting his own name and is embarrassed by this. It was not what he intended. The musical notes can be heard here and there, far away, sometimes nearby, but Linnæus has got something in his eye.

He is still holding the gardener's instrument. He is still trying to give it back. He lays it down on the garden path, alongside the borders created by the movement of the rake. Just so. Neatly. Nothing must be broken. Just so.

Linnæus:

"Nothing was added to the Creation. Nothing is being added to it. Everything exists as it was once designed to. So how can anything be taken away?"

In conversation with Linnæus, Artedi railed against the habit of giving fish animal names, calling a shark a fox or an ape, calling an angler-fish a frog.

"We should not regard fish as reflections of land animals. They have their own realm."

Linnæus said:
"You are right."
Thinking: he has already gone.

The gardener tells the children that he can make them as firmly rooted to the spot as a mountain, if they simply hold on firmly to one of their toes with one hand.

The children do not believe him and he asks if he can demonstrate on one of them. Anders steps forward. The gardener leads Anders to a tree and puts his arm around the tree, then has him pinch one toe with his fingers.

"Do you see that you are motionless. That you cannot move, other than by relaxing your fingers' grip on your toe?"

Linnæus sees the children laugh at the gardener's trick. He has to see everything.

It is dawn, on the 28th of January. Carl's name-day. The river Sävja is a thin trickle in its bed under the ice this January as the waxwings gather in the rowans, where they are exposed to a shower of hail.

The creatures, alarmed, are making themselves scarce. The horses, likewise, take fright.

Linnæus, awake, steps outside, strolls to his grove. He hangs pairs of green Kungsholm glasses as bells on the branches of an oak, an elm, and an ash in order to listen to the jingling caused by the wind when it rises. They are his Aeolian beakers, his wind-harps of glass. But this morning the wind is still, and the bells are motionless.

One glass he has saved. He pours wine into it, to the brim, and drains it to celebrate the name of the day.

Linnæus to his students:
"Whoever researches into the nature of insects finds that the so-called metamorphosis is not a *transformation* but only a *shedding*.

Artedi possessed the sharp gardening shears of logic. A tool which the gardener does not have in his collection. Linnæus makes a distinction between the realm of plants and the realm of animals. But he says there is a third one. It is the realm of stones. In his garden of plants and animals he now wants to have a ring of stone. And therefore tells the gardener to make plans for a stone fence.

The gardener replies that he knows the powers-that-be have decreed that stone fences are to be erected.

Linnæus says that his stone fence is to be erected for the sake of the garden, not because of enclosure regulations.

The gardener does not reply. He looks down at the ground. Looks out at the fields.

Linnæus says that his stone fence is to lie, not round the garden, but in it.

The gardener asks if Linnæus has seen Bielke's dike at Lövsta. The one that was erected in the autumn of the year before last. And which has already started to fall down.

Linnæus says that he has every confidence in his friend Bielke.

He says: "My highly-esteemed friend Sten Carl Bielke, Vice-President of His Majesty's Royal Court of Appeal in Åbo, who together with myself founded the Academy of Sciences."

He continues: "Baron Sten Carl Bielke, who along with myself introduced the Latin letter form into Swedish scientific writing."

The gardener replies that, in any event, Bielke's stone wall is in a lamentable state.

Linnæus says the gardener is entitled to that opinion and that, whatever the case may be, a stone fence can in all likelihood be erected passably well.

The gardener replies that a stone fence cannot be well erected at all, since when summer comes it will be destroyed by the sun, which will warm up the south side while the north side is covered in snow and ice, with the result that the stones on the south side will work loose and fall out.

Linnæus says this can be repaired.

The gardener replies that repairs of that kind are more labour-intensive and costly than building. That it would be better to erect a whole new stone fence every year at the end of the summer. That the whole countryside could devote itself to building stone fences all summer long.

Linnæus thinks that he could easily erect a stone fence in his garden himself, all on his own, if only a little one.

Earlier, there was another, smaller garden and a boy's passionate interest in names and plants.

"What's that called?" "What's that called?"

Carl walked in that garden with his father.
"What's that?" "What's that?"
His father, pleased by the boy's thirst for knowledge but tired of his forgetfulness, spoke harshly to him and issued a threat: that he would never again tell the boy the names of the plants if he forgot them after they had once been named.

"It isn't strange," Linnæus says to the gardener. "If I write 'eye', 'birch', 'perch' or 'black grouse', and the reader does not understand what is meant by these names, he will get no further with the text."

"Knowledge," says the gardener. "The brain," he says, "gradually hardens."

Linnæus is strolling and singing:
"Here comes Sir Karl. Ti-tum, ti-tum."
The gardener points to a tree.
"A pine," says Linnæus.
The gardener points to another tree.
"A spruce," says Linnæus.
The gardener points to another tree, which resembles a pine and resembles a spruce. Linnæus tries to see if the tree is a pine or a spruce.

It's an intermediate form. Linnæus is silent, unwilling to discuss this with a gardener. Such things are uncertain.

The gardener asks if the pine and the spruce haven't interbred.

"Like a horse and a donkey make a mule."

Linnæus is depressed. He has realised the magnitude of what was lost when Rudbeck's collections were destroyed in the great fire.

He tells the gardener about this.

"My father and mother and my brothers and sisters died then," the gardener says.

"I'm sorry, I didn't know," Linnæus says.

The gardener replies that he does not remember them, but that he sometimes wonders if they suffered much when they couldn't save themselves.

The gardener says he can put something in Linnæus's hand which he, Linnæus, will not be able to see, although everybody else in the whole world can see it. Linnæus cannot believe this. The gardener insists that he can. Linnæus denies it.

The gardener lifts Linnæus's left hand to his left ear and closes his thumb and index finger round the earlobe. Then he asks: "Can you see your ear?"

Linnæus wants to reply: "Is it as simple as that?" But he says nothing.

The gardener: "Everyone else can see it, but you can't see it."

The disciple Rolander is in the garden. He asks the gardener if the grass snake is poisonous, if the greenfly bites, if the crow pecks people's eyes out.

When the gardener replies, Rolander leans his head back, gazes intently upwards, and grips his nose with his fingers. The gardener falls silent.

They stand like this for a while. Then Rolander leans forward, blows coagulated blood out of his nostrils, and spits on the ground several times.

Thursday morning. There is a delivery of cheese and butter from Hallkved. Linnæus stands on top of the roof-ridge and greets the delivery with a shout. The servant and the coachman wave.

Now Linnæus sees before him all the commodities that pass him by and rejoices that he is spared them, these extravagant commodities.

He is spared sugar, confections, desserts, raisins, cinnamon, mace, almond tart, jelly, carp, oysters, caviar, any preserves, all sauces.

He is spared wines, brandy, tobacco, tea, coffee, chocolate, silks, satin, lace, drums, card-games, board-games, dice, comedies, concerts, masquerades.

He is spared offices, paintings, carriages, farm-hands, maids, wax candles, fine palaces, great windows, plaster, porcelain.

"All that makes one weak! Weak!"

The gardener, with the butter and cheese in his arms, walks towards the food cellar.

It is a cloudy winter but not cold. From Slottsbacken one can see the stinking haze over the Uppsala plain.
It is the 17th of February, late evening. Linnæus and the gardener are out in the waterlogged meadows at Lövsta. Bright moonlight. The forest hard on the horizon.

The almanac shows a minor lunar eclipse at eleven o'clock at night.

The gardener cups his hands, as if to capture something. It is a game. Linnæus guesses.

"Mussels."

Linnæus knows the gardener maintains that he has found the mollusc shells in the clay. Shells of molluscs from the salty Baltic, which stretched this far until the land rose.

Linnæus specifies.

"*Mytilus edilis*, the common sea mussel. *Cardium edule*, the cockle, with its ribbed shell. *Tellina baltica*, the little smooth one."

"Feel," says the gardener, lifting up a handful of soil to Linnæus, who takes it.

"Feel."

Linnæus rubs the soil between his fingers, the black, smooth, clay soil glossy in the white light. He says nothing.

The gardener squints at him.

"There are bullheads and turbot out here."

A little shadow passes over the edge of the moon.

"The peasants say we are out in the bay now."

The shadow over the side of the moon slowly disappears. Linnæus thinks that soon they will be rowing home.

Linnæus lets Rolander depart for Surinam in America and orders from him two hundred cochineal beetles, fifty to be females, placed on their mother plant the prickly pear, for cultivation in the orangery and for use as a colouring medium. For the improvement of the national finances.

He stands in front of the glass-panelled cabinet and looks at the things inside. He stands for a long time, looking fixedly at object after object. So as to remember them. But sometimes he spends too long on one thing and then it happens that he forgets one of the others. He gets stuck.

One must assume that he is happy in such moments, even if someone entering the room just then would see that he was not laughing.

Today, Löfling and Forsskål take their leave.

They explain solemnly that they intend to travel like the bee, collecting from many flowers, and not like the spider, which draws threads out of itself.

They walk down the slope to the ship and Linnæus sees them turn and wave.

It is the 28th of February, morning. Suddenly cold as ice. Linnæus, who has been afraid of the cold all his life, delays getting up. The coachman is waiting outside to drive him to Uppsala.

The coachman becomes impatient in the cold and knocks on the front door. Linnæus does not answer. The gardener comes to the coachman's aid, opens the door and calls up the stairs to Linnæus.

No reply from up there. The gardener, clearly and in a loud voice:

"The coach from Böksta is here. The coachman is waiting."

Linnæus finally calls downstairs:

"A good coachman likes waiting!"

The gardener, from the stairs:

"Good crayfish like being boiled alive."

Linnæus:

"The peasant recognises plants, perhaps even cows and goats do too. But which of them has any knowledge of plants?"

Linnæus returns to his home in Småland and finds that his brothers and sisters are ill. They are all in bed. Candles have been brought to their bedsides but not lit. The room has been thoroughly cleaned.

Linnæus goes up to his siblings and feels their foreheads. It is fever.

Linnæus creeps in beside his siblings and lets vapour blend with vapour, warmth with warmth, so that his healthiness joins itself to their sickness.

The fever fades from his siblings' foreheads and they get up, thoroughly rested, clear-eyed, healthy.

But the following night, the fever is there again. A more virulent fever than before and their eyes are cloudy, their bodies powerless.

Linnæus has a sheep slaughtered and flays it, laying his siblings inside the fleece to draw them back from death.

He waits. He holds the flat of his hand over their foreheads and faces. He wants to feel their breath becoming cool and dry. He wants to feel the fever leaving them.

Wind. The gardener and Linnæus are standing in the grove beside the oak, the elm and the ash, listening to the jingle of the Æolian bells.

"Glass", says the gardener, "as a material is fluid

in its natural state. At our temperature it takes on a more solid form. But it is still fluid. Only frozen. But still moving the whole time, just a little, inside itself."

Linnæus replies: "Then glass is related to the mussels in the seas. After all, they are nothing but a fine moisture which has acquired a shell."

While giving a lecture at Uppsala he holds a long, narrow strip of paper between his fingers, folded several times so that in the end it is tiny. For each section of his address he unfolds a part of the strip.

He keeps his thumb on the final part throughout. When he gets there he lifts his thumb and starts on the final section. This happens now.

He is talking about barley-toads. He says that their call is heard when it is time for the peasants to sow their barley. He describes how, in Skåne, the barley toads screeched towards evening as if great bells were ringing three miles away, although they were nearby in the ponds.

This, he says, is precisely what struck him as strange. That the creature's call, when it is nearby, can be heard far away.

The students stand silently, pondering. Billberg, Åkerhielm, Dubb, Rehn, Beckstadius, Bungencrona, Ekbom, Sandberg.

When they speak, they are from Skuttunge, Västerlösa, Levene, Norrby. He sees them slowly leaving him and returning to their parents and their farms.

Back at Hammarby again, Linnæus mentions the passage about the barley toads to the gardener. The latter replies:

"If you put a bucket over your head in the summertime and submerge yourself in a lake shouting loudly into the bucket it can be heard a long way away."

All that evening Linnæus revels in the gardener's observation. He thinks that it must necessitate an extra section and an extension of the long, narrow strip of paper for his next lecture.

But how it came about, this knowledge of the gardener's, he doesn't inquire.

Morning. The post-boy comes with a letter from Rolander to Linnæus.

"Gardener! He writes about crocodiles. He writes that anyone who is used to them can bestride one of them, put a bridle on it and ride it like a horse."

Linnæus shows the letter to the gardener. In the bottom corner there is an ink drawing of a crocodile half-submerged in a river.

The gardener:

"The artist has kept a considerable distance between himself and his subject."

Linnæus to his students, who are gathered round his table:

"When the hunt is on for a fellow who has run away and someone tells me that he is definitely in Sweden, then I know that he should be searched for in this country and not in some other one. If someone else comes to me and says that he is definitely in Småland, then I know in which province in the country I should look for him. If yet another person comes and assures me that he is in Skallelöv parish, then I know that he should be sought in that parish and not elsewhere. Finally, someone comes and says he is in this or that farmyard: then I have found what I was seeking.

In the centre of the table are an egg and a bowl of water. The egg sways to and fro in the direction of the bowl. Linnæus makes to go and investigate, but the gardener takes him by the arm.
"Wait."
The egg sways.
"Anders showed me. You blow out the contents. Put a common leech inside. Seal it with white wax. Put a bowl of water alongside."
Linnæus stands, hesitantly. Disapproving.
"Who is this Anders?"
"Anders. He is just a child."

Now and then large packages arrive for Linnæus. The post-boy hands over parcels allegedly containing strange plants, which however are only clumsy hoaxes. Linnæus is on his guard. He knows the story of the wonderful stone from Würzburg with the incised fossilised frog so incredibly beautifully outlined in it, a stone which the famous professor Beringer described in eloquent essays which later, out of wrath, shame and contrition, he had burned when it emerged that his own students had, for a joke, put together a *lying stone*.

Sometimes, too, visitors turn up, although they

tend to be genuinely odd. The gardener has the task of turning them away. He talks with them then. Sometimes for far too long and insufficiently dismissively, in Linnæus's opinion. On occasions he suspects that it is actually the gardener who has enticed them to the garden. This constant procession of charlatans, perfumers, vagrants, snake-oil salesmen, vagabonds, wizards, wise men and wise women traipsing along the highway and over the fields towards Hammarby.

Linnæus can see them clearly from his window. But at night he does not see clearly. He thinks they are standing with their faces pressed up against the panes, looking in. Like the bogeymen that mother and father used to scare him with, so that he wouldn't go out at night.

Thursday morning in April. Cheese and butter. But the servant looks pale and falls to the ground from the driver's seat, hurting himself badly.

"Certain diseases," says Linnæus, "are caused by slack fibres, others by tight ones."

The servant whimpers.

"The tight fibres can be made more pliable by a greasy preparation. The slack fibres can be pulled together by an astringent preparation and strengthened by a bitter one."

The coachman and the gardener carry the servant in.

"There are also diseases which proceed from bodily fluids and which depend on their nature or mixture. A sour nature can be cancelled out by a dry preparation and fixed by a bitter one."

The servant lies completely motionless, staring vacantly.

"Our body," Linnæus continues, "also contains the less well researched locomotive element in the bone-marrow and the brain, which sends out sensitive nerves to all parts of the body. When this element has been damaged, it depends in the first instance on the diet, which consists of breathing, ingested nourishment, movement, sleep, secretions and mental activity."

The servant suddenly vomits, then loses consciousness completely. The coachman and the gardener are greatly perturbed.

By the afternoon the servant has recovered and he drives with the coachman to Lövsta.

Linnæus is in the garden equipped with magnifying-glass, botanical pins, botanical knife, lead pencil, vasculum, unbound papers and a box of pins for mounting insects. Attire: a baggy shirt and wide trousers in sailor's style.

The gardener is curious about the book that Linnæus is wandering about with. It is *The Gardener's Dictionary* by Philip Miller, gardener and first botanist in the Chelsea Physic Garden. The book is a small, handy octavo volume designed to be carried in a garden while one works.

The gardener wants to look inside the book and tries to get close to Linnæus. But Linnæus moves off along the path, facing away from him, and calls out in a loud voice:

"This is not about kitchen herbs and decorative

plants. It is not a book for ordinary gardeners. It is a book for botanists."

Linnæus told Artedi about the apothecary Seba in Amsterdam. About his uniquely comprehensive and universally admired museum of wonders and about his blind faith in the famous and singular seven-headed hydra, taken from Prague by Königsmarck and now in the possession of the mayor of Hamburg.

"Actually," said Linnæus, "an artificial body, probably with a frame of narrow wooden ribs and filled with linen rags, which had been covered with snakeskin and provided with seven heads taken from weasels, as can easily be seen from the hydra's teeth."

Linnæus was amusing about his membership, under the name Dioscorides II, of Seba the apothecary's natural history society *Academia Leopoldino-Carolina Naturæ Curiosorum*.

It is the 23rd of May. Linnæus's birthday. Now if you must be Linnæus, you can be Linnæus. But Linnæus is afraid.

What is Linnæus afraid of?

He is afraid of finding, when he goes out into his garden, that there is no garden there.

That he will find, when he goes to look at his collections in their glass cases, that there are no glass cases and no collections there.

That is what he is afraid of.

That the twenty-eight disciples will disappear. That his brothers and sisters will disappear.

He goes out into his garden every day, with a view to holding on to it. On these occasions he supplies himself with a motive. It can be a simple one. Like watering a particular plant with the green watering can. Removing some shoots on a shrub to prevent a too vigorous growth. Keeping couch-grass at bay.

This process is profane rather than sacred. Unlike some of the disciples and certain visitors, Linnæus does not apprehend the daily round in the garden as something close to an act of creation. More like an act of management. Or perhaps it is more correct to say that the creation, from the time that God left it, has in all probability taken the form of something to be managed, with, sometimes, human assistance.

Therefore he does not stop going out into the garden to give it his attention. He thinks that if he does not go out in the garden it will wither away and disappear.

The gardener to the servant and the coachman:

"Come and see some funny pictures and figures."

He has got a large pewter dish ready and filled it with water. The farmhand and the coachman lean over it and look searchingly all over the surface.

Then the gardener strikes the surface of the water with the flat of his hand and the water soaks the servant and the coachman. They rub their eyes and are disorientated.

The gardener says:

"Now you are both funny pictures and figures."

The three of them smile. Linnæus has witnessed this. He sees everything.

Linnæus is talking about his books. How they can store all the knowledge in the world.

"How?" asks the gardener.

"By distinguishing between description and event."

The gardener stands still for a moment, then hops around in zigzag fashion along the paths, returning to Linnæus and standing still again.

"How? How?"

Linnæus continues.

"Classification does not proceed solely from nature, but just as much from human thought. It is our way of comprehending nature."

The gardener:

"I cannot imagine anything of the kind."

It is morning, the 13th of June. As the almanac had forecast, there was a partial eclipse of the sun by eight o'clock. It is dry and warm at this time and Linnæus is watering certain plants several times a day with the green watering-can. It's an effort to move.

He sprinkles a little water over his wristband and moistens his brow. He looks for the gardener and sees him sitting on the stairs by the east wing. The children have gathered round him. The gardener is gesticulating. Linnæus approaches slowly with the watering-can but is not keen to draw near and therefore cannot make out what the gardener is saying.

There is a knock at the door and the postman holds out an envelope that is flat but bulky. Linnæus signs for the letter and takes it inside. He takes off the wrapping-paper and finds two sheets of cardboard. He separates the two sheets and finds, between two leaves of tissue-paper, a dried plant. An accompanying letter is addressed to him. First come the obligatory long-winded salutations, then the message itself.

"Whatever God may have created on this earth, probably nothing is more remarkable than this flower, which is so obviously rose, lily and hemp at the same time. Not a rose, a lily and a hemp plant, but rose, lily and hemp all at once. One plant but three origins. The discovery, which is one specimen among several found, was made in a marsh south-east of Leiden by a young student called Frans van Haal and is sent by me, Anders Blecke, botanist at Leiden University, for you to marvel at and investigate."

Linnæus lays the accompanying letter aside. He places the plant on his workbench, fetches the magnifying-glass and examines the plant's parts. He very soon spots the deception. The plant has been created by human hand in that the different parts have been attached to each other with paste. He can tell from the smell which type of paste was used. He calls for the gardener and proceeds to demonstrate, with the gardener as witness.

"A stupid forgery. Potato paste. A new and excellent type of paste which I have used myself to good effect. For other things, properly."

Linnæus knows. Everything that is found on earth is created by God and no new species have appeared on earth since it was created. Nothing is new and no new species can arise by mixing together those species that were once created.

Linnæus fingers the long strip of paper.

"The air we inhale has electricity, the air we exhale does not."

But there are no twenty-eight disciples standing around him. Only the gardener outside the window in the dark. Linnæus starts again.

"The air we inhale …"

"Yes," says the gardener.

His face is quite close now, right next to Linnæus. But his voice sounds as if it was coming from far away. Linnæus tries again.

"The air we inhale has …"

"I have met people," says the gardener, "who are mainly inhalation and others who are mainly exhalation."

Linnæus feels he is under water in a lake. It's the summertime. He has a bucket over him. Yellow-bellied toads all over his body. The gardener is standing on the shore and shouting to him.

"People who have electricity! People who don't have electricity!"

Next morning Linnæus sacks the gardener and appoints a new one.

The new gardener arrives and introduces himself as Cajanus, the tall Finn. He is a giant who had previously exhibited himself for payment in various parts of Europe and who was rejected for Frederick William's Guards because he was a head taller than any other man in the whole regiment.

"Take this rake", Linnæus tells him.

But this morning when Linnæus descends his staircase and comes out into the garden, the usual gardener is standing there talking to the coachman and the farmhand. It's Thursday. Linnæus goes up and tastes the cheese and butter. The upside-down glasses are ringing in the trees, for the wind is uncommonly strong.

The students are scanning:
 "Monandria, Diandria, Triandria, Tetrandria, Pentandria, Hexandria, Heptandria, Octandria, Enneandria, Decandria, Dodecandria, Icosandria, Polyandria, Didynamia, Tetradynamia, Monadelphia, Diadelphia, Polyadelphia, Syngenesia, Gynandria, Monoecia, Dioecia, Polygamia, Cryptogamia."

The gardener wakes up in the shed. Linnæus goes over there and takes him by surprise:
 "You were sleeping."
 "It's the heavy rain. It makes me drop off and go into a deep sleep."
 "You are at work."
 "Forgive me."
 Linnæus looks along the walls. Asks:
 "What have you got in here?"
 "I call it my museum."
 "What is it?"
 The gardener gestures towards the walls of the hut and the tools hanging there. He says:
 "There are sometimes very strange flowers in this garden."

Linnæus, thirsty, at the well, fills the scoop with water and drinks greedily, drinks it dry, fills the scoop again and drinks, fills it yet again and drinks, slower now, waits for a moment, looks around, drinks it dry and fills it again, his thirst slaked now, but goes on drinking water.

The children have gathered round the gardener. Linnæus approaches and hears him telling them about centaurs. There are giants and monsters and gods and heroes, says the gardener.

Linnæus thinks that the gardener wants to include him in the audience, yes, that his words about monsters have a special subtext.

"The children ask me things", says the gardener. "I tell them."

"What you, gardener, call monsters are flowers and plants which have their origins in normal forms. Any forms other than those originally created by God do not exist."

"Then what's this?" says the gardener, leading Linnæus to a strangely-shaped ranunculus which most certainly is not recorded in the *System*. "Does it exist or not?"

Linnæus replies:

"Gardener! The poet has a need to enlarge and to diminish. But in reality everything has its correct size. The poet also tries to join together elements from different quarters in order to create new fantasies. One such is your centaurs. The horse and the man are natural forms in the world of nature. But centaurs do not exist in reality. They exist only in the imagination. Your ranunculus is at first sight something unique, distinct. But if you look more closely you will see that it does not constitute a new species but is only a variety of its kind."

The gardener says:
"But mules and hinnies exist. I've seen them."

The disciples Sparrman and Thunberg depart.
Early July. Night. No wind. Warm. Linnæus wakes up and can't get back to sleep again. He hums a song in an attempt to become sleepy. What were the words? "In artless repooose …, in artless repooose …"
Like this, from the start:
"Two friends were sitting …"
And finally:
"What disturbed them? – Raaa-iiin."
Linnæus does not sleep again that night. In the morning he goes out and leads the gardener to the plant that was used as a demonstration.

"It so happens," Linnæus says to the gardener, "that the Creator has allowed nature a sort of sense of humour. Accordingly, there are two differences between plants. One of them is a genuine difference. It is the diversity brought about by the infinitely wise hand of the Almighty. But the other difference, which expresses itself as variations in the outer shell, is nature's work in a momentary jest. This is what you, gardener, know how to exploit. I therefore distinguish between the Almighty Creator's species, which are genuine, and your abnormal specimens. The former I regard as being of the greatest significance for their Author's sake. The latter I reject because of their Author. The former exist and have existed from the beginning of the world. The latter, which are monstrosities, can boast of only a short life. Your monsters will have no descendants."

The children run to and fro over the Uppsala plain. They move around as a group, here and there, just as the mood takes them. Linnæus is standing motionless, balancing on his heels, looking out of the window at the children. Understanding nothing. He seeks the assistance of the Italian terrestrial telescope. Then he spies the dragon. The dragon is puffing here and there over the Uppsala plain and the children are running after it. It is high up, it is sailing well, it swoops like a swallow, it pounces furiously down towards the children but turns aside just in time, Linnæus holds his breath, the dragon climbs, it drifts sideways and gets caught in an oak-tree. Stillness. Linnæus takes a step to the side and breathes out.

The children arrange themselves around the oak. Linnæus wants to go down and tell the gardener to help them. He looks out over the garden and notes that the gardener is being thrown here and there. It's the wind.

Dry leaves cling to a wall. Linnæus feels the glass of the window-panes, which are bending inwards. He wants to wave to the gardener. But the gardener is preoccupied with his own affairs.

Linnæus:
"There are varieties so different that although they are of the same species, botanists have assigned them to two distinct species, such as *Polygonum amphibium*, water knotweed, because in water it floats, whereas on land it is erect or a climber."

Linnæus warns the botanists about their tendency to see varieties as new species, whereby the number of plant types is increased too much, insofar as no boundaries are observed.

Linnæus to the gardener:
"You are the person in the middle and I am on the fringes."
The gardener:
"I can't understand something like that."

The students sometimes ask Linnæus to tell them about his trip to the north. Linnæus is reluctant on these occasions. The students take his reluctance as a hero's modesty at the mention of his feat. But Linnæus knows that his reluctance is for another reason.

He is especially embarrassed when the students want to hear about the journey from Sörfold to Malmströmmen.

Linnæus is the only person who knows that it never took place.

The same with Kaitum. He was never there.

But the students want him to describe again the swift-flowing melt-water streams which forced him to depart from the path and wander barefoot in perilous swamps, or to walk in a state of undress through the cold melted snow.

Linnæus tells the stories, ashamed of how animated his performance can become. It is not that he regrets the untruthfulness. There were reasons for it. But he is worried that he has introduced something into the world that was not there before.

Now it is there, and it is his fault.

It's a civil day, Linnæus says to himself.
 Meaning: an unusual sky, an amazing heat.
 "It's odd," Linnæus says to himself.
 Meaning: the laws of life, the star system, the development of the butterfly, the night.

The disciples Osbeck, Adler and Hasselquist depart. The gardener shows Linnæus a leaf from a maple-tree. On it are a number of black spots of varying shapes with yellow edges. The gardener knows that there is a parasitical fungus that attacks maple leaves. He holds the leaf close to his ear and listens.
 "Fungi are strange," he says. "You don't know what they do. You don't know if they are animals or plants. You don't know anything."
 "*Rhytisma acerinum*," says Linnæus, after a while.

Linnæus creeps into a tunnel. The tunnel is forbidden. Elbows. Mud.
 Stones. He exists. The prohibition exists. His knees. There is no sun in the tunnel. His knees. It is forbidden to speak. He remembers the sand. It is forbidden to move. He remembers his hands. It is forbidden to think. Tears. He remembers the tunnel. His knees. The prohibition holds. Sand. Stones. He is not there. But the prohibition does not always apply. Him. His hands. But the prohibition can apply at any time. His knees. Stones.

It is the 23rd of July. The dog days are here. Linnæus

is standing in the garden, sweaty, dazed by the heat, and thinking about the stone fence he has ordered to be erected. Out there, in the fields, are the goats that come into his garden at night, laying waste to it and fouling it. He finds it strange that, according to the regulations, it is the owner of a farm who is responsible for fences. Surely it is the beasts' owners that should be fenced in, not the farms.

The gardener:

"At Lövsta the goats climb right up onto the stone walls. They're made for the mountains. On Bielke's lands the stone wall is the wildest, steepest thing there is. The goats want to be there and their wandering to and fro loosens the stones."

The wife of Pastor Corvin in Skanör showed off her discovery of an egg within an egg. The smaller egg, a hen's egg like the larger one, was as small as a musket ball and on being opened it was found to contain only egg-white, no yolk.

Several eyewitnesses saw it, as the egg was opened up at breakfast. Linnæus remembers their jocular speculation as to whether another egg might be found within the egg that was inside the egg, and so on to infinity in ever smaller forms.

Linnæus has a sense of unease when he remembers this and feels unsure of the cause of his unease.

Linnæus arranged for Artedi to travel to Amsterdam. 3,000 fish in the collections of Seba the apothecary to order and describe. It was the second distinction.

Linnæus adopts a reproachful tone and warns his friend, in jest.

"Don't swim too much in the canals!"

The students occasionally ask Linnæus to tell them about his time with Boerhaave in Holland, especially the story of the Swedish whitebeam.

Boerhaave pointed out a tree in his arboretum which he declared to be a curiosity, not yet described by any naturalist. Perhaps an addition to the Creation? Linnæus immediately recognised it as our common Swedish whitebeam, *Sorbus intermedia*.

Boerhaave disputed this.

Linnæus then told him that Vaillant had given a detailed description of the species in his *Botanicon Parisiense*.

Boerhaave disputed that too. He said he possessed that book and had carefully studied its contents. The book was sent for and it emerged that Linnæus was correct.

Linnæus likes telling this story. Boerhaave had claimed to have found a species outside the System. But Linnæus had shown that it was already there, named and clearly described. Nothing had been added to what already existed.

The beginning of the month of September. Three nights of frost. The frost threatens to damage the Indian cress, the marigolds and the Turkish beans.

The gardener lays blankets and covers over his plantings.

Black terns are in the thick sedge in the alluvial mud along the Funbo, Lagga and Sävja rivers. Linnæus sketches their plumage of black velvet with a blue-grey cloak around it. At the base of the beak he notices a red, rapid movement.

Where the gardener has been sitting, Linnæus finds small fragments of cork, and asks the reason why. But he receives no answer or he does not remember the answer. Linnæus feels weak. The extremities of his hands and feet are numb. He takes a needle and presses the point against his skin, but feels no pain. Instead he experiences pricking sensations in his hands and itching and crawling along his forearms. Tip of the nose cold.
Linnæus is with his siblings. They are ill. Pale. A fragile, whispering unease surrounds them.
Linnæus:
"Where does it hurt?"
His siblings' slow gaze:
"In my side."
Linnæus:
"Can you say where?"
"In my side."
His siblings make a gesture. An arm, a hand, a wrist, an elbow, rises slowly and sinks back.
"Which side?"
"In my side. In my side."
Their exhaustion. Linnæus creeps down beside them in the bed, up against them. Their shoulders and necks are warm, their plaits thick, their hair neatly combed. Their noses and knees, their temples,

waists. Linnæus in bed with his siblings in order to draw the fever, the sickness, out of their bodies.

"They're shellbacks," says the gardener.

Linnæus looks at the little statuettes lined up in the middle of the path. They are little trolls, jolly little figures. The gardener carves them out of cork and dresses them in shells he has found. They have faces and anyone who looks at them feels he wants to talk to them. Linnæus wishes he could make something of the kind himself and gives the gardener due praise.

October now. Linnæus calls the gardener over.

"I've taken on Nietzel. He will be the chief gardener. You will be his assistant."

"Very good," says the gardener.

"Dietrich Nietzel. He is Georg Clifford's head gardener at Hartekamp."

"Very good," says the gardener.

"He has 3,000 species under cultivation there. He is bringing about three hundred plants with him. The cases are on their way and should be here in three days."

"Very good," says the gardener.

Hybrid. It is hubris. Arrogance. An affront to God's laws.

That a hybrid creature should be found among plants, as with animals?

That out of two separate types of plant a third should emerge, like the mule from the horse and the donkey?

The likelihood of such potential hybrids' independent propagation?

"It is still uncertain," says Linnæus.

In the night Linnæus sees from his window twinkling lights, flashes, white reflections, inexplicable, in the leaves of the Indian cress. They are inexplicable because there is no external source of light that could cause such a light-effect.

On being asked straight out, the gardener says he saw the lights too, but without bothering about them since after all he couldn't fit them into any context.

Linnæus is concerned that the business with the Indian cress be properly investigated, so that an explanation is found for what happened.

Thursday morning. Delivery. There is a rumour about the large menagerie at Hammarby. It is a rumour which started with the gardener's comments to the coachman and the servant from Hallkved about the large number of animals that had to be looked after in the garden and the dwelling-house. It is a rumour that has spread to Tjocksta, Vallby, Sävja, Krisslinge, Edeby, Söderby and Ängeby in Denmark parish in Vaksala hundred, to several farms in Funbo parish in Rasbo hundred and to Kasby and Marma in Lagga parish in Långhundra hundred.

A cockatoo, several peacocks, a cassowary, several

civet cats, four kinds of parrot, a number of small apes, an agouti, two ant-eaters, a racoon, several goldfish in the pond, and, if the servant and the coachman are not mistaken, several other animals besides of a strange but unknown type.

Many stories are woven around these animals, in particular the last-mentioned unknown ones.

Whoever creeps up to the house and peers in through a certain window will be able to see a young orang-utan which always sits stock-still, and which some regard as life-threatening and some suspect is stuffed.

Close into the house, the whole neighbourhood knows, there can also often be heard hoarse, loud voices, frightening, making the blood run cold, as if they were coming from the throats of ghosts.

On this Thursday morning the coachman and the servant linger behind longer than usual after handing over the butter and cheese to the gardener. They ask the gardener warily what the truth is about all the stories that are circulating.

The gardener says that there are three parrots. The cry of "It's twelve o'clock, Mr. Carl!" that is regularly heard comes from an elderly parrot which expects its lunch at that time. Another parrot is behind the cry of "Come in!", which takes visitors by surprise when they hear it in the entrance hall.

But the strangest cry, the gardener says, comes from a parrot which is in the habit of shrieking, in a harsh and piercing voice, "Blow your nose!", but only to one person, viz. Lövberg, when the parrot comes across him in the garden.

At this point in the gardener's testimony, Linnæus

had drawn near with the intention of getting a piece of cheese. He heard.

"Who is Lövberg?"

The gardener replies:

"He's my old assistant, who lives in the shed among the rakes. He sleeps most of the time but works well and sometime you must meet and have a chat together."

Linnæus doesn't go into the garden, but out in it. For him it is not a mollusc, not the inside of an egg, not a cave. It is not a hiding-place.

It is the water the mollusc lives in, it is the hollow in the sand where the egg is hatched. It is the rock face outside the cave. Everything is visible there and he must see everything.

One morning Linnæus becomes aware of raised voices coming from the gardener's shed. He approaches, cautiously, to eavesdrop and hears strange cries.

"Swine strikes!"

"Cuckoo sticks!"

"Inn passes!"

"Hussar strikes!"

"Rider passes!"

Linnæus can make out the voices of the servant, the coachman and the gardener. There are also a few other voices. It's like a chain. It goes round, it's fast and unbroken. "Cuckoo sticks!" "Inn passes!" "Rider passes!" "Swine strikes!"

Linnæus does not understand.

It is night. Linnæus, unable to sleep, has gone out into the fields. He looks straight up into the sky. There are stars there but no pictures. He presses his chin down against his chest, bends his back, bends his knees, collapses, turns round and comes up again. It was a somersault and Linnæus feels heroic and pitiful.
Thursday. Cheese and butter. But the coachman comes alone. The servant is not with him.

"It's this business with the pastor," says the coachman.

He looks distraught.

"With ..?" asks Linnæus.

"Rudqvist, the new pastor. Dead. Beaten to death."

"And the servant?"

"They're looking for Petter. He's in hiding."

"Is he guilty?"

"The pastor borrowed a horse from the stable, without Petter's knowledge. Drank a few jars of panacea first."

"Snaps?"

"Yes, coffee with a dash of snaps."

"And then?"

"The pastor rode to Lövsta. Dahlqvist said that he and Bielke played backgammon and had a few nice tots."

"Snaps?"

"Yes, but without getting the worse for wear. Then they rode home. But didn't get there. In Gunsta they saw him sitting perfectly still on his horse. Then nobody knows. But Petter fled when they came looking for him. Rudqvist's body was found in Funbo lake, by the bell tower. No sign of the horse."

"What do you think?"

"Rudqvist was drunk and wandered around, fell in the lake. The horse will come back. Petter too."

On certain long afternoons Linnæus imagines that he is telling children, in the shadow of an oak, about how he cultivated pearls in the River Fyris, about the stubbornness of the leaf-rolling beetle and about the marvellous herbaceous plants of Arabia Petraea.

Linnæus is sometimes afflicted by extreme feelings of distrustfulness and thinks that the twenty-eight students wish to destroy him. He confides in the gardener, who counsels:

"Ask the most foolish of them."

Linnæus wonders:

"But foolishness does not own the truth."

He receives the answer:

"If you find yourself in a circle of cunning men who all wish to have you where they want you, turn to the foolish one who doesn't have the wit to be treacherous and you will get to know the truth."

The gardener:

"How can you believe the world was created? It was actually there from the beginning."

November, a Thursday morning, after All Saints' Day. Snowfall. Delivery. The coachman is not there. The servant at the reins. Linnæus comes down to get a bit of cheese.

"Petter! You're back!"
"I know what I have and haven't done."
"Where is the coachman?"
"Andreas has gone. He's a wanted man. But he's not guilty. I can't believe it."
"And the horse?"
"It's all right."
"What have you done with the cheese? The butter?"

Linnæus takes the cheese and the butter in his arms.

"It's true," Petter says, "it's true that Andreas drinks. He's gloomy. He drinks to cheer himself up. But it's for the sake of being happy. Not anything else."

Linnæus knows nothing about the servant and the coachman and the pastor. Linnæus notes that snow crystals become smaller in very cold weather.

The 28th of January. It's Carl's name-day. Linnæus lectures, happy.

"We are like electric lights," he tells the students, "with which God illuminates his theatre."

Linnæus is standing in the garden planning the Siberian Garden, around which, to protect against the goats, a stone fence needs to be erected. With single or double courses of stone? It's worth thinking about.

The gardener arrives and is informed of the plans. He says the enterprise is pointless as far as the vigorously climbing goats are concerned.

Best with two courses, Linnæus thinks. The first one well buried in the ground, then large blocks of stone in two columns. Between these, plenty of small stones, supporting them and binding them together.

"Earth sows," says the gardener. "That's what they have at Lövsta. Lots of earth sows."

Linnæus does not understand the gardener.

"Why are you talking to me about pigs?"

At such a moment there is a tremor in the air between them. Linnæus is Linnæus and the gardener is the gardener, they both know that, and it's usually straightforward between them. Yet at such a moment something gets in the way.

But the moment passes. The gardener adds, without a tone of didacticism: sows in the earth are what the locals call pebbles, the smaller stones that are used for infill between the blocks.

On top of everything the flatter slabs.

The man in work-clothes comes with a plank on his shoulder, stops and lifts his hat.

"My name is Kristoffer Hörner, watchmaker. I'm building myself a house over on the slope. I wish to announce myself and my services in case they may be of use. If you have broken timepieces I will put them right for a modest payment. And new ones can be had at a reasonable cost.

Linnæus is careful to say a polite thank-you for the offer and asks if he may return to it if the need arises.

The man expresses his thanks, equally politely.

"Come and see the house one day."

February. March. Lectures. There are genera, families and species. But the students are unable to differentiate between these orders and varieties, which are relative. They seek to classify in terms of place of growth, the size of the plant, spots on the flower, the form of the stalk, the colour of the root.

Linnæus explains to them that the System has to call a halt somewhere.

"Varieties are insignificant deviations."

He explains that a boundary must be set between the fixed System and the variable varieties.

"Otherwise there would be no end to the discipline."

He forbids the students to devote themselves to the varieties.

The gardener is telling Linnæus a story:

"There was a man who locked seven goats in a hut. The goats died of hunger in the hut. The old boy didn't go there until after seven years had passed. Then the old boy fell ill and lay sick for seven years."

Linnæus:

"Why are you talking to me about goats?"

It's early April.

"Here," says Lövberg to Linnæus, "is the cuckoo on the branch. Here is the hussar on foot with his sabre drawn. Here is the boar hunted by the hound. Here is the mounted horseman, banner held high. Here is the inn with its sign, a wine-glass. Here is the wreath. These are real laurel leaves, not oak leaves.

Here is the flower-pot. Here is the fool, watch out for him. Here is the joker, he can have any value whatsoever."

Lövberg has laid out the little coloured cards in rows on the ground. Linnæus picks up one of them, examines it. Lövberg, politely:

"It's the pot. The flower-pot."

Linnæus looks hard at the card. It's a garden. In the background a pyramid and a low building with Corinthian columns. In front of it stands a lady with a straw hat, and a postillion. A garden urn between them. A barrier of stone in the foreground.

"The card is very worn," says Linnæus.

"We play a lot."

"Why do you shout?"

"Because we're playing."

"Why is the lady there and why is there a stone wall in the way?"

"We just play."

"Where is this garden?"

"I don't know. I've never thought about it."

Linnæus picks up several cards and turns them over, one after the other. On one of them there is something printed on the back in tiny letters. Linnæus can't see well enough to read them. He hands over the card to Lövberg and asks him to interpret it.

"Klinckowström's, it says."

"Who is that?"

"It's the manufacturer. In Stockholm. The one who printed the cards."

Night. Linnæus, out in the fields, shouts:

"Aster! Rosie! Velvet!"
Listens, but nothing happens, no answer.
"Beauty! Proudie! Missie!"

The gardener takes Linnæus to a place far away from the garden and shows him some plants. Linnæus recognises them. They are *Alopecurus nigricans*, creeping meadow foxtail, which loves the salt of the sea.

But the gardener and Linnæus are on flat meadowland far from the sea.

"It's the salt source rising up," says the gardener.

Linnæus wets a finger and tastes.

"Here, underneath us," says the gardener, "is the bottom of the Baltic."

A morning in June. A knock at the door. Linnæus opens it, and there is a youth standing on the stairs. In his arms he has a wooden box, the top covered with a cloth. Linnæus recognises one of his students, a native of Roslagen, poor but clean and industrious, if no genius. His name is Ziöberg.

Ziöberg lifts the cloth and says he has found a plant in his home district that he has never seen before and which he is unable to classify. Linnæus invites Ziöberg in. The plant is lifted up and placed on the table.

Linnæus studies it and at first suspects that Ziöberg is lying about where he found it and that the plant has instead come here from Japan, Peru, the Cape of Good Hope or some other distant place.

Ziöberg insists that he picked it himself in his native district.

"I found it at Södra Gåsskär."

Linnæus still suspects that Ziöberg is telling lies. That he has pasted an alien inflorescence into the plant with the intention of setting his teacher a test.

It emerges, however, after Linnæus has examined the plant with a botanical knife, that such is not the case. No artificial combination has taken place. But Linnæus does not need any lengthy study to describe the plant decisively as a common *Linaria*, even if it is rather odd in its outward appearance. It's sufficient, actually, to smell it.

"A common toadflax. Fly-flower. Good for haemorrhoids."

The thread-like, creeping root and the round, foot-high stem and the stalkless, lancet-shaped leaves are entirely consistent with *Linaria*, as are the taste and the characteristic smell. Linnæus admits that the resultant plant's tight cluster of flowers near the top is clearly different, but this – he assures Ziöberg emphatically – is to be understood as a trick of nature and nothing more.

"The habitat can hardly have any more examples to show and no second generation is possible."

"Crystals," Linnæus says to the students, "are stones whose properties are so completely distinct from other stones that we have not yet heard of anyone who has been able to fathom how they are connected. I have therefore been exceedingly troubled and perplexed trying to fit them into their correct place in the System, for either the most precious metals ought to be brought together in one ranking with the basest ones, or they should be spread throughout the System, thus dividing up Nature. I have made minute observations in this matter and thereby sought to base my opinion on such findings as can be established without fear of contradiction. I am now certain that crystals should be assigned to the *Salia*, although the usual response is that they cannot be assigned there as they neither taste like the salt family nor can they, like salt, be crystallised. Everyone applauded my System until they came to the crystals. Then they said, open-mouthed, that I had gone wrong, that I was clutching at straws. But if one pays heed to my observations, the matter is clear.

Strong sunshine. Towards midday at the beginning of July. Linnæus is lying in bed with a migraine. It's not the sloe-wine, nor the cold, strong winds, but a severe disappointment.

A package comes from Rolander. It's the cochineals from Surinam. They have been carefully placed by the disciple on a Barbary fig in a pot to send to Linnæus. But Linnæus is on an excursion with the students. The gardener takes delivery of the package from the post-boy, unaware that Linnæus has sent for the insects. He therefore cleans off all the dirt, and in consequence also the rich abundance of insects, the red males, the white females, pulps them between his fingers, tosses them out into the garden with cries of disgust, then puts the plant in a fresh vase.

In the evening Linnæus is searching for the grubs in the garden.

The gardener is standing beside him with a lantern

in his hands to illuminate the ground. There are waxwings all around them, replete with the little creepy-crawlies from Surinam.

Linnæus takes to his bed, going over and over in his mind the moment when the gardener greeted him cheerfully:

"A weird thistle has arrived from Rolander. But ugh! It was so full of vermin."

Many days pass. Early one morning Linnæus is on the bank of the river Sävja. He is in his nightshirt and skullcap, which is sewn together from six strips of red velvet. It is still, windless. The slow-flowing water is completely covered with a fine, light-yellow membrane of pollen. He makes his way down to the water's edge and squats down, bends over and carefully lays the flat of his hand on the surface. The pollen does not stick to his skin but simply clusters together a little in the water.

He stands up, takes his things off and walks out into the river. He lies on his side flush with the surface, lets his legs drift slowly in the water and his arms move alternately to and fro with his hands cupped like bowls. *He is swimming.* He keeps his head above the surface and sees how the yellow pollen is squeezed away from him. He is in the middle of a circle which is dark against the light, clustered pollen. The circle remains round him when he swims, very slowly, against the current to where the Sävja has its source in the meeting of the Lagga and Funbo rivers.

There he clambers out, shivering in the early morning, and walks back along the water's edge to where he left his clothes. Much later, at home, on going to bed at night, he notices that yellow pollen has stuck to the hairs on his body and dried in. When he rubs his hand over his arms and thighs a light mist forms round him in the room.

At night, when Linnæus hears the goats coming into the garden, he goes down and drives them away from the flower-beds with powerful whip-lashes. The goats flee, without making a sound, but no sooner is Linnæus back in bed than he hears them in the garden again.

Only after he has sought out the gardener in his shed and instructed him to chase the mischievous beasts away is the garden left in peace. When the gardener strikes the goats they set up a high-pitched wailing, as if in anguish over a protector's punitive power, and rush off in the direction of Lövsta.

"Everything that exists," says Linnæus, "is a question of size and proportion. An artist may wish to alter this. But the Creation made everything in the correct size. If our eyes were microscopes, every human being would look like a masked scarecrow. All the lineaments of the face as rough and coarse as if seen through a burning-glass. A skin full of scurf, ringworm, pimples, boils, blisters, pustules, scabs, lumps. There is no word from Nietzel. The cases with his plants fail to arrive. Linnæus makes no comment.
Linnæus with his siblings. He wants them to do as he does. He shows them.

"Follow me! Do as I do!"

But they turn away, find something else.

He races after them, collects them together.

"Say after me! Copy me! Then it'll be fine!"

But his siblings walk away from him, in different directions. They want to do other things than those he has thought of, have their own interests.

Linnæus runs after them, grabs hold of them, one by one, imprisons them in dungeons he has built, binds their ankles and wrists with coarse ropes he has plaited and fastens the rope through iron rings he has forged and which he has driven deep into the metre-thick walls of the dungeon.

"Do what I'm doing!"

But his siblings get up and leave.

"Look how I do it and repeat everything! Don't do anything else!"

But his siblings are already far away from Linnæus.

The post-boy comes with letters from Artedi in Amsterdam. Linnæus misses his friend and expects him to complain about his exile and loneliness.

But the letter is full of positivity and energy. Linnæus feels pleasure at his friend's pleasure, but also a degree of sadness. As if someone close to you had disappeared for good. Which was the case.

Linnæus reads his friend's lengthy report on his work on the large manuscript about fish.

The tone of the letter is cheerful: "Confirmation: one can swim in the canals!"

The stone fence has been erected, with difficulty. In his Siberia Linnæus plants Alaska wild rhubarb, Siberian peony, Mongolian sedum, wild tulips, magnificent skullcaps and Siberian aster.

He waters them with the green watering-can.

It's night-time. Linnæus has been wakened from his sleep by the gardener and led down to the garden.

The gardener is holding a torch before him. He has placed a vessel with liquid in it on the ground in front of them. He is talking eagerly, as if in a hurry:

"You can put out fire with water. But I know a water that burns. I can take the water out of beer wort and leave the essence of it behind, the bit that burns. Look!"

The gardener touches the torch to the liquid and it flares up.

Linnæus takes a step backwards so that his coat isn't scorched by the flames and he sniffs the air to identify the substances that are burning.

"*Aqua ardens*. Burning water. I use it to put my preparations in. An excellent medium for conservation. Boyle kept a human embryo in such a liquid for fifteen years. One problem is the yellowish clouding of the object. But that is outweighed by the advantages."

Thursday morning. Linnæus is waiting. Hörner arrives. He says that the delivery has been cancelled. The coachman and the servant are being searched for. They have disappeared.

"It has to do with Petter's wife. Anna Cathrina."

"Yes?"

"She's dead. She was ill."

"In what way?"

"Three days before her death she was violently sick after eating a sandwich with grated cheese. She complained of a severe headache and convulsions. She had recovered by the following day. But then the day before her death she was sick in the same way again after drinking a cup of coffee. She vomited up the coffee. But the pains got worse. She didn't recover again. She died. They opened her up. She was pregnant. Her stomach contained a dark-grey, slimy mass. In it they found small white grains which had a sharp smell and gave off a white smoke when they were burnt on the embers."

"Arsenic," says Linnæus.

"That," says Hörner, "is just what I heard."

Linnæus listens to him. But knows nothing about the servant, the coachman and the coachman's wife. Has nothing to say about them.

Linnæus, at his window, looks up at the night sky. It is light, it's that time of year, and the stars seem to be smouldering. But Mars can be seen on the horizon, utterly calm.

The 3rd of August. There is a hammering on the door. Morning. Linnæus opens up. It is the student with the rare plant which Linnæus was able to assign to the *Linaria*. Ziöberg. In his arms he has a very large covered box. Linnæus shows him into the kitchen, the box is placed on the table. Ziöberg lifts up plant after plant. He says nothing. Linnæus lays them alongside each other, one after another and begins to examine them very attentively.

His teacher's silence alarms Ziöberg, who fears an outbreak of rage and introduces his defence.

"I found them on Södra Gåsskär on a hillside some distance from the first habitat. There are others. The whole slope is full of them."

Late August. The goats seem to relish the Siberian peony and the Siberian aster. At night the Siberian garden is full of goats.

The days pass. Autumn. Smell of rusty nails in the cold mornings.

It's the 10th of October. Linnæus hasn't done this before. But he knows what is going to happen. He covers all the windows in his room. He uses several layers of wallpaper. He is careful not to let any light in.

When he has observed that the room is completely dark he cuts a hole in the fabric. The hole faces onto the garden and is about a decimetre in diameter. The sun is blazing outside and a thick ray penetrates into the room through the hole.

With a fine mirror bought from Björknäs he directs this ray to a screen which he has draped with the white reverse side of the fabric. He looks at the upside-down picture that has appeared on the screen. It is a round surface, a circle with a dark, flickering field inside, something that moves right through, something darker, small. And on the edge of the ring of light something white, the sky.

Linnæus knows that the dark field is the gardener. He lays his hand against the screen, the back of his hand against the fabric, the palm of his hand catches the light and the dark field moves in his hand, he closes it, but the dark field moves over his knuckles and wrist.

Linnæus paints the screen with a strong, porridge-like solution of spirit and lime, but the image will not stay still.

He tries to capture the contents of the ring with a fine pen. But his drawing only amounts to a few strokes over which the movement of light continues.

In a series of attempts, one after the other, he daubs the screen with different liquids. With iodine, paraffin, brine, zinc chloride, boric acid. With a number of different solutions of arsenic of differing degrees of acidity. With rosin derived from pine resin, formalin, glycerine, solution of sugar, mercury chloride and carbolic acid.

But the image won't stay still.

He tries a combination of alum, cooking salt, potassium nitrate, potash, acid of arsenic and water, which after being warmed has glycerine and methyl alcohol added to it. But the image does not stay still.

Finally he runs down the stairs and out into the garden. He shouts for the gardener to come up to the room. But the gardener is not there.

Linnæus runs to the grove and shouts, but is alone in the grove in the midst of the leafless trees in the wind.

Winter, and already the 28th of January. It's Carl's name-day. Biting cold.

Linnæus goes out into the garden with a chart showing the berries and fruits of summer in pretty colours. Brown cherries, pears, blueberries, raspberries, strawberries. The children gather round the chart and admire the pictures of berries and fruits.

Linnæus wonders:

"Does cold result from the particles which otherwise create warmth standing still? Or is cold an active capacity which has the power to draw together and cause rigidity?"

The children imagine eating the berries and fruits.

A planned garden must have a heath alongside, a field that is not cultivated, as otherwise the actual garden would not emerge as cultivated.

But in addition, beyond this heath one must imagine an area which is to the heath as the heath is to the garden.

If such an area was inhabited, Linnæus thinks, its inhabitants would be four-footed, dumb and shaggy.

They are *homo ferus*. They live blind and silent, knowing nothing of us.

Occasionally one of them strays over to us and we can investigate it.

Linnæus is keeping a book about this.

The bear boy, *Juvenus ursinus lithuanus*, 1661. The Lille girl, *Puella transisalana*, 1717. The Pyrenean boys, *Juvenus ovinus hibernus*, 1719. The Champagne girl, *Puella campanica*, 1731.

He looks out the window. Are they playing cards in the shed?

A peasant, Linnæus thinks, is more like an ape than a courtier.

With the students. The paper strip. The thumb.

"I reckon as *Petrificatum pictura assimilans* all the kind of things that are simply a polite gesture to those who make such a fuss about fossils. I have seen large cabinets overseas full of fossils which cannot reasonably be assigned to any particular system. But if I should exclude them, although they are nothing more than nature's jest, I would draw upon myself all the wrath of their admirers."

The twenty-eight students. A quarter of a hundred. Sala. Sorunda. Nyland. Viby. Paper strip in hand, thumb on the last place.

"They are generated when vitriol water gets between the lamellæ of a slate that has cracked, after some plant or animal has crept in there and rotted, for then the water inside crystallises and is transformed into a dark figure with the help of the mould. Rarest of all in this system is *Lapis geographicus*, which has points and lines representing a geographical table."

He sees everything and he has to reflect everything. Therefore he continually changes and expands the *Systema naturæ*.

The fourteen folio pages in the first edition.

The two thousand three hundred pages in the twelfth edition.

Everything must progress through him. Nothing must be lost.

February. A knocking at the gate. The person knocking introduces himself in Latin. He is Mr. Missa, a

Frenchman. He has letters of introduction from Haller. He wants nothing more than to be a disciple of Linnæus.

Linnæus receives him in the tricorne doctor's hat which is dressed with light-green silk taffeta and decorated with a pink silk band.

"Gardener!" he shouts. "This is Mr. Missa, my first pupil from France. He has fled from Buffon and come to us to learn botany."

"Take this spade," says the gardener to Mr. Missa.

Linnæus is in an excellent mood:

"Virgil says that the task of the brave is to spread their renown through their exploits."

The gardener:

"Hippocrates says that experiments are dangerous."

Linnæus is on the edge of the garden, near the field. He sees a lady with a straw hat in the distance. A dog wanders around, stops and barks. A sow, several sows, come up out of the ground, like small spheres. Everything is soaked from a chamber-pot. A post-boy appears.

"Herr Carl! Herr Carl!"

Night. A knocking at the door. Linnæus goes down the stairs with a candle in his hand. He opens up.

In the light from the candle he sees a weary, bloodless face, round and childishly questioning with an open mouth and searching eyes. Linnæus recognises his disciple Rolander and asks him to step in.

Rolander hesitates on the step, doesn't say a word, stands swaying, seems to be on the point of falling asleep.

Manages to get out, after a while, in a faint voice, that he has come to retrieve his cochineals.

Says in addition that he is there on behalf of the others. He begins to gabble – sometimes inaudibly or barely audibly – a list of names, familiar to Linnæus.

"Burman. Næzén. Acharius. König. Torén. Lenbom. Acrel. Söderberg. Martin. Adler. Kähler. Sparrman. Solander. The brothers Afzelius. Hallenberg. Alströmer. Bartsch. Löfling. Tuwén."

Rolander falls silent, becomes shy, takes a step backwards, as if he expected some protest. But continues with his gabbling of the names.

"Dryander. Berlin. The brothers Gardell. Bierkander. The brothers Alströmer. Falck. Montin. Forsskål. Gahn. Hasselquist. Kalm. Ödman. Thunberg. The brothers Hagström. Rothman. Osbeck. Pontin. Tärnström. Wänman. Åmann."

Rolander tugs at Linnæus, drags him out into the garden and gives him a hard poke in the chest. They both fall headlong to the ground.

Rolander's cry, in a very loud voice:

"Where are they? Where are my cochineals?"

Linnæus is lecturing.

"Everything has its place in creation, even in the realm of stones. I assign *Petrificatum quadrupedis* to the *Zoolithus*, *Genus 8:um*. It is rarer than anything else seen in the System and has no other use than that one can say what such a thing is called when it appears. I give it this name for the convenience of those who love to see the wonderful variety of Nature."

Dim light, muffled sound, many suspicions, nothing happens in the open, patient waiting, feeling of threat and promise mixed. What is it in him that knows? He does not see it. His eye is a dark room. It depicts objects, but he sees nothing of the affected nerve. The nerve goes to his brain where he sees nothing. But there is something that perceives what he is unable to investigate.

Far to the south, in Hartekamp, unnoticed, a carriage and horses is getting under way. It is Dietrich Nietzel, who, toiling, full of dread, is beginning his journey.

An unaccustomed warmth in April, with warm afternoons, when any movement would be intrusive in the stillness.

On such afternoons, after working on the paths and plantings, it is the gardener's custom to sit down on a bench with a little table in front of him. He places his instrument on the table and begins to play.

When the sounds reach Linnæus's window, he usually comes down and asks the gardener to tell him how the instrument came into his possession and how the sounding-board comes to have seventeen strings.

Linnæus also usually asks the gardener after a little while to explain how the relationship between the melody strings and the drones is to be understood and why the latter cannot be shortened.

After a while, Linnæus also usually asks why the cross-strings are moveable and whether the instrument is called a zither or a dulcimer.

On just such warm afternoons, when the gardener is playing his instrument, the watchmaker Hörner also usually comes and listens. On these occasions he never says anything, simply listens very intently.

Herr Missa throws Lövberg out of the shed and moves in himself. Herr Missa has no money. His level of knowledge is modest. Or his ignorance is infinite. His temper is appalling. He demands regular meals with hot food. He continually proclaims how thoroughly tired he is of the whole business of botany.
Watchmaker Hörner walks along the road with a plank on his shoulder, stops beside Linnæus, who is standing by the gate pondering his stone fence.

Linnæus doesn't know what to say.

Hörner says:

"Come and see the house one day!"

Then goes on his way with his plank.

Linnæus asks his siblings what it was like to die.

"Dear Carl. At first we began to get a whistling in our ears, then we became short of breath, as if something heavy had lain on our chests, then a giddiness, next a thick mist in front of our eyes, after that flashing as if someone had lit gunpowder, and moreover as if someone had fired guns right at our ears."

Linnæus wants to lie down beside them and draw

the fever out of them with his body. But it is too late. They are already outside themselves.

It is the 23rd of May. Linnæus's birthday. The children have made a wreath of flowers for him. He tells them that when he was a baby his hair was as white as snow.
It is a very warm afternoon. The gardener is sitting in the garden with his instrument. Linnæus has come down and posed his questions. Watchmaker Hörner has come to listen. He has another guest besides. Hörner introduces him as Herr Norlind, organist.

Herr Norlind listens to the gardener playing. His enthusiasm is great and the gardener, pleased by this response, extends the moment into a little concert, an afternoon concert in the heat. Herr Missa joins the company, taking notes. Lövberg stands a little way off, with a rake in his hand.

After the concert, for after all it must finish sometime, Norlind delivers a little speech in which he praises the gardener's playing. Despite being widely-travelled he has never heard anything of the kind before and he would like to describe the gardener's playing of the instrument as almost perfect.

In fact, there are only two things that he would personally like to draw attention to with regard to this hummel – as the instrument is properly called, he says – and that is two notes which are very slightly wrong. But this could very easily be corrected . "How?" asks Linnæus. "Perhaps it would be easiest if I showed you, says Norlind, with the gardener's permission?"

Norlind now sits on the bench with the instrument in front of him and adjusts the cross-string on the sounding-board.

"The basic scale is a major one," he says. "But you have to avoid the fourth being too high and the seventh too low. It's only a question of a millimetre. A trifling little millimetre, here ... and here ... and here."

Linnæus is proud of his gardener. After Hörner and Norlind have left them he grasps the gardener's hands and cries out:

"Gardener! Gardener!"

It is a light night out in the field, in the mud. Linnæus alone, in a central point from which footprints radiate out in every direction. The prints are from walkers' boots. The walkers have taken rapid strides. They are the prints of all the disciples. They followed him, he went in front, they followed in all directions and now he is alone in the centre.

Dawn and sunrise over Lövsta. Moisture covering the ground. Linnæus is surrounded by his cows. Their breath is thick steam in the morning chill. They are Summer Rose, Beauty, Maidie, Aster, Proudie, Dainty, Lily, Rosie, Blossom, Thrift, Mumsie, Missie, Velvet, Goldie. They graze their way towards him. Nobody sees him among them.

He is lecturing. On the table in front of him is a specimen of *Linaria*, Common Toadflax, and a specimen of Ziöberg's remarkable plant.

"They look identical. This one, which is known to us, has four paired stamens of unequal length and a single spur. But this other one, which is hitherto unknown, has five spurs and five stamens of equal length.

He demonstrates, compares. Four additional spurs. An additional stamen. A significant addition. The circle of students around the table.

"It comes from *Linaria*. And yet we must see it as being from another, as yet undescribed species, even belonging to a different class from *Linaria*. To me, it was common toadflax. Now it is not common toadflax. It has made the leap from Didynamia to Pentandria. I call it *Peloria*, from the Greek word "pelor", which means malformation or monster. Nothing can be more fantastic than what has happened with this plant of ours, namely, that a misshapen offspring of a plant, which formerly produced irregular flowers, begins to generate regular ones. In so doing it deviates not only from its maternal family but totally from the whole class. It is no less amazing than if a cow gave birth to a calf with a wolf's head."

Linnæus looks up from the table at the circle of students. They are motionless, silent. Linnæus imagines they are astounded. He continues:

"We are confronted with the astonishing conclusion that new species occur within the world of plants. That genera which differ in their organs of reproduction can have the same origin and nature. That different organs of reproduction can be found in the same genus. As a result, the fundamentals of reproduction, which are also the fundamentals of all botanical science, would be overturned. The natural classes of plants would be exploded."

Strong wind. Linnæus with case in hand on the Uppsala plain, waiting to depart, lifts the case high into the air.

"Take it!"

But nobody takes it.

Lövberg in his shed, drunk. The gardener is thrashing him.

"You are a swine, Lövberg."

Lövberg screams from the pain of the blows, but his screams turn into the grunting and shrieking of a pigsty, then into fits of laughter, then into improbably solemn tones. A story begins, narrated by Lövberg.

"Listen to this. When King Louis of France was ill, no-one in his court could get him to utter the slightest laugh, however much they joked and played the buffoon. One jester after another approached him to practise their arts, but while the gentlemen and ladies of the court laughed themselves silly, the king sat apathetic and stony-faced. No-one could think what to do. But then in came a particularly resourceful jester leading a troupe of trained pigs, bizarrely dressed-up and dancing and skipping to the music of a bagpipe. And the king laughed! Now, gardener, what do you say to my little story?"

The gardener has listened patiently. In certain circumstances Lövberg has a talent for telling such stories.

"It's only a fairy-tale, Lövberg. You made it up. I can hear that, for you tell it like a fairy-tale."

"And you won't forget it, gardener. It exists now, you'll never get rid of it."

"You're a swine, Lövberg, a swine. It doesn't exist,

it can't exist, any more than there is a ... a crazy countess just because I'm standing here thinking of a crazy countess!"

"There you are, gardener. Now there's a crazy countess as well! Swine and countesses everywhere!"

Night. A figure is down among the paths. Linnæus looks down from his window. A man is leaning backwards and gazing up at him. Spitting. It's Rolander. His nosebleed.

Linnæus goes down, calls his name. Rolander clears his throat, spits, wipes his nostrils with his fists, rubs them against his coat, excuses himself, and pleads that he comes with greetings.

Linnæus carefully takes his time, pronounces different names, enquires after their health. Rolander replies:

"Sparschuch? Fell downstairs, dead. Wetterman? Burnt to death. Grufberg? Cut his throat with a razor, dead. Baeckner? Died of fever in Paris. Lutteman? Still living, insane. The Ferber brothers? Both died in poverty in America. Gisler? Mad, murdered three people. Edvall? Buried in Canton. Berzelius? Died on the way home from China. Lindh? Died on the ship *Terra Nova*. Lundberg? Died of fever in Stockholm. Carlbohm? Died of consumption in Paris. Björnståhl? Died of plague at Litochoro, Greece. Lundborg? Drowned. Salomon? Drowned. Luut? Drowned. Wennerberg? Drowned. Söderberg? Drowned."

It's early June. The watchmaker is standing by the coach talking to the coachman and the servant. Linnæus sees him helping himself to a piece of cheese. Linnæus comes down and follows suit. The cheese is very good. They stand together chewing it. It's pleasant in an unaccustomed way.

"There are three kinds of cheese and butter," the watchmaker cries.

There are lots of kinds, thinks Linnæus.

"There is then, there is now, there is afterwards," says the watchmaker. "But everything happens at once. You took a piece of cheese then, you're eating it now, and you're wondering what will come afterwards. But that was then."

Linnæus begs pardon for the obtuseness of his thought processes, which means that he doesn't have the right kind of receptiveness for such flights of fancy.

The watchmaker balances his plank on his shoulder.

"Come and see my house at a convenient time."

Linnæus is talking loud and clear.

"The total number is there, gone over so many times, put in order. And then this single one comes along which changes everything. One plus one plus one plus one, I know what that comes to. But this latest addition?"

The gardener to Linnæus, standing a short distance from him.

"Can you see me properly where I'm standing?"

"Yes. Of course I can see you."

The gardener comes closer:

"It's true. As you can see, I am visible. You are also visible. But I can make myself *invisible*."

"How?"

The gardener is right beside Linnæus.

"It's foolproof magic. I will exist, just like now, I will see everybody, but no-one will be able to see me, even if I was standing in the middle of the church."

"How?"

The gardener walks around and begins to explain in a matter-of-fact tone:

"All I need is a barrel. I bore lots of small holes in a barrel, creep down into it and shut the lid from inside. Through the bottom, which will be turned upside-down, that is, pointing to the sky, I will be able to see everybody through the small holes. But will be *invisible* to all!"

In every one of his copies of *Systema naturæ* Linnæus scores out in black ink the words "no new species emerge".

Linnæus is acquainted with lots of gardeners. Jakob Gottschalk and Henrik Kralitz in Lyon. Johan Snippendal and Herman Cornelius in Amsterdam. Philip Miller in Chelsea.

But none of them is like his own gardener. It would be wrong to say that he is acquainted with him. Wrong too to say unacquainted.

Yet Linnæus knows him inside-out. He has always been there.

It's Sunday, and Linnæus is resting and repenting.
On Monday he cancels man and woman.
On Tuesday he takes back the cattle.
On Wednesday he lets the birds and fish disappear.
On Thursday he cancels everything to do with the reptiles and insects.
On Friday he sees to it that the stars, sun and moon disappear.
On Saturday only the stones on the ground are left. He cancels them too.

Linnæus is sick. His hands and feet feel stiff. He feels his veins are swollen. He has a sensation of tension in his muscles.
On this warm afternoon the usual things do not happen. The gardener leans back on his bench. He has his instrument in front of him, but he is not playing it. Simply picking with his fingers at a little ball of sticky soil. Clayey soil.

Linnæus comes anyway, enticed as much by the silence as he had formerly been enticed by the playing, and asks:

"Is it a dulcimer? Or a zither? Or a hummel?"

Then ceases his questions when he sees the gardener's eyes, which are not eyes but two small, cold balls of clay.

I wonder if the fungi should constitute a new natural realm of their own, a *regnum neutrum* or *chaoticum*.
"In Skåne," says Linnæus to the gardener, "I saw the body of a dean who had been dead for eleven years.

It had been treated with alum, not with pitch, and also with vitriol, and in addition it had been filled with the ears of hops so that the result was exceedingly true to life."

The gardener stands silently.

Linnæus continues:

"But the most wonderful thing would be if one could discover the art of melting amber and insert the dead body into the melted material, thus preventing the body from rotting."

The gardener silent.

It happens after this that Linnæus traces with his finger over the gardener's forehead, along the lines that are there, up to the hairline and down over the eyebrows. There can be no response to this deed.

All that can happen is that Linnæus withdraws his gesture, takes a step to the side and lets the moment pass.

Warm morning. Still June, long-drawn-out June. There is a knock at the door. It is Artedi. His friend on a visit. He talks about his life in Amsterdam.

"I go to the tavern from three to nine, work from nine till three in the morning, sleep from three until noon. That's the whole story!"

Linnæus wants to ask about the canals, but doesn't ask. He feels unsettled, insecure, although he is the host and his friend is the guest.

Artedi has brought his manuscript with him and reads from it all night for Linnæus.

Artedi stands with a fish in front of him, a strange fish. Linnæus has never before seen an example of this species. Artedi dissects it, cutting out the relevant parts quickly with a sharp little knife, releasing the organs while he demonstrates:

"*Anableps tetrophthalmus*, popularly known as the "telescope fish" or "four-eyed fish". It is distinguished – *look here!* – by the fact that the outer row of teeth is flexible and consists of soft teeth, while the pharyngeal teeth, *here!* are pointed like the teeth of a carding comb. But the most distinctive thing is the structure of the eyes. The hemispherical cornea is divided by a horizontal strip of conjunctiva into two halves, an upper and a lower, *here!* and the pupil too is double due to an interlacing of the iris. The upper halves are designed for seeing in air, the lower ones for service in the water. In such a way the fish can be on the waterline and with the help of these two pairs of eyes it can see just as clearly over the surface as under it."

Artedi places the two organs of sight in Linnæus's hand.

"This fish was caught on a muddy sandbank in Guyana."

Linnæus thinks he and his friend are singing: "Two friends were sitting / In artless repose, in artless repooose …"

But they are not singing. Artedi goes on to the next fish, a megrim caught in the Trondheim fjord.

It begins to rain heavily outside. Artedi doesn't let it disturb him. He lifts up the megrim and holds it in front of Linnnæus's face. Opens and shuts the mouth.

Artedi has departed from the garden, is on his way back to Amsterdam. Lövberg comes looking for Linnæus:

"He left this with me, to hand over to you after his departure.

Linnæus studies the plant, which is growing in a pot. There are some smaller plants there too. An attached label reads: *Hort. Cliff.89.* From Clifford's garden.

Even the original source is given: *Habitat in Libano.*

Linnæus can see that the plant belongs to the umbellates. But he has never seen this species before.

Linnæus shouts:

"Gardener!"

There is something he wants to relate, to assert, to exult over. But the gardener looks worried and it all dies down. The gardener shows Linnæus the palm of his hand. In it are a mass of black blotches of different shapes, yellow round the edges.

"I don't feel anything," he says.

Linnæus sees how the blotches are creeping inside the cuff of the gardener's shirt.

"Nothing," says Linnæus.

It is meant as a question, a question in response, but he can hear that it does not sound like a question.

"I don't feel like raking any more just now," says the gardener. "Not raking. Not just now."

Still June. Linnæus is out in the fields. It is night. He is calling:

"Beauty! Proudie! Lily! Blossom! Goldie! Summer Rose!"

But nothing happens.

Lövberg arranges a beating for Herr Missa, who then disappears from Hammarby. Linnæus summons Lövberg to his room and thanks him.

"A rascal may play his part as well as he likes," says Linnæus, "but in the end he has to pay."

Lövberg answers that he will also gladly convey a thank-you to his assistant.

"Your assistant?"

"Broberg. A smart fellow. He lives in the shed among the rakes. You will certainly get a chance to see him one day."

Linnæus, sick, screams loudly with pain, throws himself on the floor, runs here and there, as if burnt by fire, bounces off the walls. His mouth is twisted, his tongue is lacerated by his teeth, he suffers from intermittent loss of vision.

It is a dark night. The Swede wanders home from the apothecary's table at Haarmlemmerdijk near Brouwerstraat to the room on Warmoesstraat by Nieuwebrugsteeg. He is between being drunk and feeling sick. There is nothing in sight. By the sides of the bridge over Herengracht a slight chill can be felt. It is the clammy haze that comes off the water and touches the skin of passers-by. He feels an impulse to throw up. A rusty iron pillar serves as a support. He continues on his way, in a good mood, relieved.

A purity in the air. Sunrise within an hour.

Broberg is whistling a tune. He is painting the shed green. But he is not painting green. He is painting moss, verdigris, blades of grass, mildew.

He paints the door of the shed white. But he doesn't paint white. He paints graupel, arsenic, sail-cloth.

He changes his mind and paints the door yellow. But he doesn't paint yellow. He paints butter, urine, straw.

Linnæus is standing at the window looking out at Broberg and listening to the tune he is whistling. Then tries to whistle it himself.

Artedi dead.

Found at dawn, cold and drowned.

Linnæus out in the garden with the students. Magnifying-glass, lead-pencil. On the ground is the pot with the plant from Artedi, the umbellate from Lebanon. Lövberg with spade, digs a square. Linnæus to the students:

"The umbel on top. The flowers in the middle without sprouts. The fruit consists of small rough scales."

Linnæus writes on the label which is fastened round the stalk. Lövberg finishes digging and steps to one side. Linnæus goes down on one knee and places the tall plant and the smaller plants in the soil.

"We shall give it the name *Artedia squamata*, the scaly one. From *Arabia petræa*."

Lövberg waters it with the green watering-can.

It is the smooth linen and the creases that become visible in it, the four legs of the bed, the three pillows by the head, it is by the foot of the bed that he is standing for this one action, the tossing, to toss, and see how it comes down, the two possible outcomes, heads or tails, and he tosses, and it comes down, and he tosses again, and the coin falls on the smooth linen and the creases appear, and then it is as if a decision has been taken, but there is the clock as before and the lamp, the magnifying-glass, the wallpaper, and on the floor the feet which are his and which hold up the body that tosses the coin, up, up, falls.

Then an animal comes pacing, strides straight out of a trap, climbs out of the iron ring of the snare. It is a bear - cunning bears, to keep their dens secret, walk backwards for long stretches, and can then hop three or four metres to the side to avoid their pursuer.

There is a knock at the door. Rolander comes in, pale, exhausted. He sits down, pleading faintness. Linnæus gives him a drink. Rolander reels off:

"Adler, dead of fever on the coast of Java. Bartsch, dead in Surinam. Berlin, dead at Delos in the bay of Guinea. Falck, cut his throat with a knife, then shot himself in the head with a pistol, dead in Kazan, southern Russia. Kähler, half-lame in Italy, got home, eventually, on foot, still alive. Forsskål, dead of fever in the mountain village of Jerim in Yemen. Martin, one leg amputated, in the north, among the icebergs, still alive. Hasselquist, dead of consumption in the village of Bagda near Smyrna. Solander, dead after a brain haemorrhage, London. Löfling, dead of fever in a missionary station in Merercuri in New Andalusia. Torén, dead of complications after a trip to the East Indies. Tärnström, dead on the island of Pulo Candor off China, aged thirty-seven."

Linnæus:

"And you yourself?"

Rolander leans his head back and presses a handkerchief to his nostrils:

"Home, deranged, after a short time in Surinam."

Linnæus is afflicted with nervous spasms. His bloodvessels are turning blue. A violent pain begins to affect his muscles. His arms are suddenly drawn in towards his mouth. His fingers are bent towards his palms. His eyes swivel in opposite directions.

"From my mother," Linnæus says to his disciples, "I have a hardy nature, but from my father, a sickly body."

He feels them lifting him high on their outstretched arms and giving him three cheers. They look up to him, praise him, give him sloe-wine, strawberries and cream to eat.

July. Slowly, very slowly, Dietrich Nietzel is moving northwards through Sweden. Through the ruins of the old castle of Axevall, past stones inscribed by the Swedish Goths, over Bråvalla heath, past the Hallenström waterfall.

It is, out of the darkness, a clarification that is being prepared, a change waiting to happen. From inn to inn he travels, asking the men of learning in each place about Linnæus and his garden.

Early this morning Lövberg has prepared the large vat with brine. He has emptied in the big sacks of salt and added the boiling water from the cauldrons and then stirred it with the large wooden forks until all the salt dissolved in the water and the brine was saturated.

Now they have taken up their places by the large table in the dining-room. Lövberg hands him the curved iron instrument. Linnæus introduces it into the gardener's nostrils and pulls out his brain, sometimes in very small pieces like worn thread-ends, sometimes in rather more connected rope-like pieces. Then he makes an incision in the left groin and takes out the intestines from the abdomen. After that he makes an incision in the diaphragm and takes out the contents of the chest, apart from the heart which is allowed to stay untouched where it is. Finally, he cuts away the nails from their beds and saves them in a box of entomological needles.

Lövberg and Linnæus drag the gardener's body to the vat and immerse it inside. They take care to place the body in such a way that the head and body do not come into contact with the brine.

His siblings pause for breath and let fly at Linnæus:

"Stop following us! We're big now and can look after ourselves. Don't you understand that we're living our own lives now and have nothing to do with you?"

"I only want to know if you are all right," Linnæus replies. His voice is friendly, gentle, but he cannot suppress the tone of knowingness and authority.

"The best thing you can do is stay away from us. You seem so anxious the whole time and we can't concentrate on what we're doing."

"I just want to make sure that nothing bad happens to you."

"You are actually just a nuisance. We sometimes wish you would take yourself off on another of those long trips."

Linnæus is the giant in which the dwarves carry out their silent work.

Their relieving each other over and over again.

Linnæus keeps to his room for ever longer periods, not going out into the garden. He sleeps late in the morning and does not wish to be disturbed.

This morning, nevertheless, Lövberg and Broberg decide to disturb him. They knock on the door. They want to announce Ziöberg, the student from Roslagen with the remarkable flowers. He is here again now with a large carton. May he come in? It would surely break the monotony for Linnæus?

Linnæus replies that he does not wish to meet the student, he wishes to be left in peace.

Prolonged bouts of vomiting and recurrent expectorations of sticky slime, repeated fits, tremendous sweats. Marked anxiety, fast pulse, copious bleeding from the gums.

Linnæus:

"What if a large number of creatures, so *tiny* that they are invisible to our eyes, are still unknown to us?"

Broberg comes looking for Linnæus, complaining about his servant young Hörner, the watchmaker's son.

"If I plant something," says Broberg, "he steals it and hides it. If I give him a pot-plant to look after, he kills it or sells it. *Adonis capensis* gone without a trace. The same with *Potentilla rupestris*. If I ask him about it, he says it rotted away. Where is *Magnolia*? And where did *Bocconia* get to? But if I forbid him to plant, he plants. Boxwood planted in my absence. *Antholyza cepacea* set out against my wishes.

This is not some story being told in retrospect, it has not happened before, he is not standing around afterwards and looking back, it is right now, it is of the moment and may vanish with it. Hörner goes up to him, lifts him between two fingers and puts him in the watch-case.

Around him are the cogwheel, the mainspring barrel and the fusee. At intervals of a minute, balls are sent gliding along a winding track. A block of wood is led down a sloping board, then turns around and wanders up, then down, and so on without stopping. The din is awful.

It is August, with traces of chill in the air. Early this morning Lövberg has laid up a supply of linen rags.

He has kindled branches and twigs to make a slow-burning fire. He has extracted resin from pine-trees and steamed out the turpentine so that only the rosin is left. Then he has used the fire to melt the required amount of rosin, which he has saved in a pan. He has emptied out the brine from the large vat. He sees that the outer skin with all its hair has come away from the body. It can drain away.

Lövberg and Linnæus drag the body out to the garden and lay it on the rack over the fire to dry out. Afterwards they leave it lying on the rack while they fill some of its cavities with linen rags. They finish off with clay and sawdust. Then they use glue to fasten the nails they have saved to the nail beds.

Then they take the linen rags, immerse them in the pan with rosin and swaddle the body layer after layer. Sometimes they sprinkle a little salt in between. Then it's ready. Lövberg wheels the figure to the shed in the wheelbarrow.

Linnæus is afflicted with palpitations and fainting-fits. Tip of the nose cold. Sweats. Racing pulse.
Linnæus with the twenty-eight disciples.
"The sea has its own stones, plants and animals, like the earth, but there are many types where it is difficult to decide if they are stones, plants or animals. The corals are situated on the border of all nature's realms, so that one is unsure where to assign them. When Marsilia was about to sketch the corals, as long as he saw them under the water they resembled flowers. But when he pulled them up out of the water they looked like stones.

Linnæus with the students. Mild, calm.

"Slates divide like pages in a book when they are split and they are opaque. They are generated by marshy sludge that has become compacted and pressed together under the water. As a result it ends up lying horizontally in flags. This is also the reason why it is found to contain primitive fish and other creatures which have been left behind in the sludge when the water-level dropped, and have thus been incorporated into it.

It is the last time. But the twenty-eight students are scattered to the four winds.

Under Linnæus, in a water-filled cavity, swim the cave fish, colourless, slender, elegant, blind. They swim without ever bumping into the rough walls. Into them disappear all the names, devoured in a trice.
Lack of imaginative power. Lack of memory. Insensitivity to touch.

Impaired vision. Declining hearing. Declining sense of taste.

Loss of speech. Declining sex-drive. Declining sense of hunger.

Deficient ability to tense the muscle-fibres. Declining sense of thirst.

Linnæus says loudly and clearly:

"I cannot look after myself."

Wind. Suddenly, October. Linnæus exerts himself to go out, led by Lövberg. Linnæus is wearing his nightshirt and the red velvet skullcap.

They stand in the grove by the oak, the elm and the ash to listen to the jingling of the hanging Aeolian bells of green glass. But no sound can be heard. They think the jingling is being drowned out by the whistling of the wind and go right up to the bells. They perceive the swaying of the leaves, each and every one of them. But from the glass bells they can distinguish only a muffled sound, dry and short, quite dull, like wood against felt.

Lövberg unhooks one of the bells and holds it up to the light. It was formerly clear and completely transparent, but is now hazy, smudgy, watered. When Linnæus looks very carefully he can make out within the material fine grey threads stretching round the whole surface.

"The glass has stopped," Lövberg says. "It's the glass disease."

He moistens one of his fingertips and rubs the rim of the glass. There is no sound. He flicks a finger off the side.

"They will not be saying any more. They have stopped."

The days go so quickly. It is the first Sunday in Advent. Linnæus is supplementing Artedi's *Ichthyologia* with a new genus under the name of *Silurus*. It contains the sheat-fish, the strange one with the large, gaping mouth which Artedi omitted in his taxonomy. Linnæus writes down the species name *Silurus glanis*.

Thinks that Artedi would have been pleased with it.

What's left behind. The records of the cows. The posthumous manuscripts. The herbariums. The stones that the students let fall when no answer comes from the teacher regarding the stones' origins. For lift me, my God, from the dust to yourself for a moment to see how you order the way of the world, what the cause is of all the wonders that happen here. The winter continues.

Linnæus devotes himself to micro-organisms:

"They have a free and simple body. They can be brought back to life. They lack outer limbs and sense-organs."

He creates a series of new classes of micro-organism, named *Hydra*, *Furia* and *Chaos*.

His illness is a little compartment which is quietly integrated into him.

The 28th of January. It's Carl's name-day. Lövberg holds his hands and feels the coldness of his fingertips.

Give me a drink, Linnæus wants to say. But says: "To Ti! To Ti!"

Yet Lövberg understands. Linnæus has his own words in place of the usual ones. He has forgotten all the usual ones, one after the other. Thrown them high up. First, the nouns. *Monandria* and *Tetradynamia*, gone. Buttons, buttonholes, waistcoats, gone. Weasel, fish, knife, cheese – gone.

Lövberg mentions some well-known people's names.

Linnæus nods, then says, clearly and lucidly: "Yes."

But when he has to repeat the names, he is unable to, and instead writes on Lövberg's slip of paper: "Can nothing."

Lövberg names Odelius, Grisell, Kyronius. Linnæus nods. Lövberg writes the names on a slip of paper. Linnæus points to the names, nods, writes: "Can nothing."

When Lövberg strikes up the first verse of some psalm, it sometimes appears that Linnæus can sing it. He does not keep in tune, but he sings the verses distinctly and fluently.

Now and then he also pronounces certain prayers in time, as it were, in an exalted and clamorous voice.

But now Linnæus is saying nothing but: "To Ti! To Ti!"

Lövberg gives Linnæus a drink of water.

February. March. The days pass. It will soon be spring. Young Hörner, in Linnæus's sickroom, paints a black raven on his wall. Hörner secretly makes a hole in the wall in the picture of the raven and thrusts a frog inside, then puts paper over it. One morning when Linnæus in better spirits Hörner shows him his painted raven. When Linnæus praises him for the handsome picture Hörner takes a candle and holds it in front of the hole. The frog feels the heat and croaks non-stop. Linnæus thinks it is the cawing of a raven coming from the picture and is mightily astonished.

Hörner is quick to give Linnæus an explanation of what has happened, to highlight the cleverness of the joke. But Linnæus does not hear the explanation. He hears only the voice of the raven.

Linnæus now perceives a non-existent ringing sound. Linnæus now perceives a non-existent visible object. Linnæus now perceives a non-existent spinning motion. Linnæus now imagines some non-existent evil in his solitude.

Lövberg, Hörner, Broberg stand around his bed. They have rakes in their hands. On their feet are boots covered in soil.

The 13th of April. Maundy Thursday. Report to George Clifford at Hartekamp, signed by Dietrich Nietzel, Hammarby, Sweden.

"All his limbs and organs, particularly his tongue, the lower extremities, and the bladder, are paralysed. His speech is rambling and unintelligible. He cannot move from the place where he is sitting or lying without help, he cannot undress, eat, or perform the least of his needs. Of his organic life only the breathing, the digestion, and the circulation of the blood are still in reasonably good order. Everything else is more or less destroyed. He seems to be totally unaware of both past and present. There are only a few servants here. Garden in the worst state imaginable. Goats wandering about loose. My work is going to require great exertions and is already begun."